BL: 3.0
AR Pts: 1.0

MVFOL

D0481661

FIELD TRIP MYSTERIES

The Zoo
with the
Empty Cage

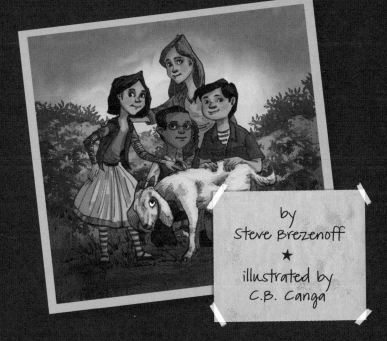

by
Steve Brezenoff

★

illustrated by
C.B. Canga

STONE ARCH BOOKS
www.stonearchbooks.com

Field Trip Mysteries are published by Stone Arch Books
151 Good Counsel Drive, P.O. Box 669
Mankato, Minnesota 56002
www.stonearchbooks.com

Copyright © 2010 by Stone Arch Books

Library of Congress Cataloging-in-Publication Data
Brezenoff, Steven.
  The zoo with the empty cage / by Steve Brezenoff ;
illustrated by C.B. Canga.
      p. cm. — (Field trip mysteries)
  ISBN 978-1-4342-1610-6
  [1. School field trips—Fiction. 2. Mystery and detective stories.] I. Canga, C. B., ill. II. Title.
  PZ7.B7576Zo 2010
  [Fic]—dc22
                      2009002574

Creative Director:
    Heather Kindseth
Graphic Designer:
    Carla Zetina-Yglesias

Summary:

Edward G. Garrison, better known as Egg, is pretty excited about the Science Club's field trip to the zoo. They'll get to see a rare display of Island Foxes, an endangered species. But when the club arrives, they learn that the foxes have been nabbed! Can Egg and his friends find the foxes?

★ TABLE OF CONTENTS ★

Edward G. Garrison

A.K.A: Egg

D.O.B: May 14th

POSITION: 6th Grade

*This can't be correct.
Please confirm.*

INTERESTS:

Photography, field trips

KNOWN ASSOCIATES:

Archer, Samantha; Duran, Catalina;
and Shoo, James.

NOTES:

Ms. Stanwyck encourages Edward's
passion for photography, but some
teachers complain of the frequent
use of the flash.

*Is photography allowed in school? I will
look into this.*

CHAPTER
ONE

My name is
Edward G. Garrison,
but you can call me Egg.

7

Yup, Egg. Like the things you scramble for breakfast. Anton Gutman, our class bully, says people call me Egg because my brain is scrambled, but he's wrong. It's just my initials: E.G.G.

That's why my friends call me Egg.

My best friends, Gum, Sam, and Cat, and I are the closest friends in sixth grade. It feels like we've been friends forever. But we only met this year in science club, actually.

Cat is the only one of us who really likes science. She's a big-time animal lover, and science is the only class where we learn about animals.

Cat joined the science club because she wanted to take care of the club's gerbil, Mr. Herbert.

Sam — whose name is short for Samantha — loves all those police shows on TV. You know, the ones where special cops solve crimes using science. So she joined the science club hoping to learn how to take DNA samples or something. She says that's called forensic science.

The science club member who really doesn't fit is Gum. He completely hates science class. In fact, the only reason he joined at all is because Mr. Neff, the science teacher, made him join.

See, Gum was causing trouble on the first day of science class this year. The punishment was to join the science club for at least a month. Once Gum became friends with the rest of us, he decided to stay.

And why did I join? Extra credit! Every member of the science club gets extra credit on our science grades at the end of year.

I'm going to need it. I'm always busy taking pictures during class, so I often miss what Mr. Neff is trying to teach.

Science isn't my favorite subject. Art is. I love photography.

But science club isn't just where we all met. It's also the scene of one of our biggest mysteries ever. See, my friends and I solve a lot of mysteries. Most of them happen when we go on field trips.

This really big mystery started one Wednesday. That's the day that science club always meets.

Gum, Sam, Cat, and I were seated at the round table in the science room.

We were a few minutes early, and our new club advisor, Ms. Marlow, wasn't there yet. None of us knew Ms. Marlow very well. She had only started a week earlier.

"So, what do you guys think about Ms. Marlow?" Sam asked in a whisper.

Cat smiled. "I like her," she said. "Did you see her T-shirt last week?"

Gum laughed. "You mean the one with the panda bear on it?" he said. "I knew you'd like her."

Cat nodded. "Of course I do," she agreed. "That panda bear is the logo of a group that protects animals, and I love animals."

I got up and snapped a quick shot of my three friends at the round table. They all smiled.

Just then, the door to the science room opened. We all turned, expecting to see Ms. Marlow.

Instead, we saw our arch nemesis: Anton Gutman.

CHAPTER TWO

A NEW MEMBER

"Anton!" Gum said. He jumped out of his seat. "What are you doing here?"

"This is the science club meeting," Sam added.

"And we all know you don't like science," Cat pointed out.

Anton smirked. "I like science," he said. "In fact, I love science. It's my favorite subject."

Anton took a chair and pulled it over to the big round table. He flipped it around and sat in it backward. "So," he said, "let's talk about planets or bugs or something."

Cat said, "Anton, stop goofing around. Ms. Marlow will be here any minute."

"I'm not goofing around," Anton insisted. "I'm joining the science club."

None of us could believe it. Anton Gutman was a troublemaker and a cheater. Why would he want to join the science club?

Before we could figure out what Anton was up to, Ms. Marlow strolled in. "Hello, students," she said.

"Hi, Ms. Marlow," Cat replied. "Um, where is Mr. Herbert? I'm supposed to feed him and water him. Plus I have to clean his cage today."

Ms. Marlow turned to Cat. "Are you in charge of the gerbil?" Ms. Marlow asked. "I didn't realize. I brought him to my apartment to care for him."

Cat's shoulders sagged. "You took him home?" she asked.

Ms. Marlow smiled. "I did. I'm sorry, Catalina," she said. "It just broke my heart to think of Mr. Herbert at school by himself at night."

Cat nodded, but I could tell she was sad about it.

"I'll bring Mr. Herbert in on Wednesdays for science club from now on," Ms. Marlow added quickly. "You can visit with him then. And maybe you could take him on a weekend sometime. Would that be nice?"

"Yes," Cat replied. "That would be nice."

"Anyway," Ms. Marlow went on, "I have two pieces of news today. First, we have a new member."

Anton leaned back and stretched.

"Do you all know Anton?" Ms. Marlow asked. She frowned. "Anton will be with us for the next four weeks because he's having some trouble in science class."

Anton laughed.

"I knew you weren't here because you wanted to be," I said, leaning toward Anton. "This is a punishment!"

Anton smirked.

"I hope my other piece of news will cheer you up, Catalina," Ms. Marlow went on.

Cat sat up straight.

"As you know, the Science Club goes on a field trip every year," Ms. Marlow said.

"This year we have a special treat. We are going to the ZOO!"

Cat squealed. "Yes!" she said.

Ms. Marlow smiled at Cat, then continued, "And even more exciting, we'll be the first to see a special new exhibit. The zoo recently got two Island Foxes."

Gum raised his hand. "I heard about that," he said. "They're — what do you call it? Engaged."

Cat laughed. "Not engaged," she said. "That means getting married. Island Foxes are endangered!" She reached into her bag and pulled out a magazine. She flipped through the pages. "Look," she said. She held up a photo of two animals. "These are Island Foxes. Cute, aren't they?"

Ms. Marlow nodded. "They are cute," she said. "The two at the zoo were recently captured in the wild."

Sam raised her hand. "Don't some zoos help endangered animals?" she asked.

Ms. Marlow nodded. "Yes," she said. "Some zoos capture animals to keep them safe and help them have babies."

Anton leaned over Cat's shoulder. "They look like ugly dogs to me," he said. "With funny short legs."

"It says here that Island Foxes live in California," Cat said. "They eat bugs, mice, fruit, and lizards. Gross!"

Anton laughed. "This isn't a very good punishment!" he said. "I get to go on a field trip."

Great, I thought. *The best field trip of the year, and Anton's coming.*

But the trouble hadn't even started yet.

THE CRATE IN THE VAN

The real excitement started the next week. The next Wednesday, after the three o'clock bell rang, the science club members met in front of the school.

"Where's the bus?" Gum asked, looking around.

I shrugged. "It's not here yet, I guess," I said. The four of us looked up and down the street. No bus.

Just then, a big white van pulled up. Ms. Marlow hopped out of the driver's seat.

"Okay, kids," she said. "Let's head out to the zoo."

We all turned and stared at Ms. Marlow. Quickly, I snapped a photo of the van.

"Um, are we going in that?" I asked.

Gum looked at me. "Don't we usually go on field trips in a bus?" he whispered.

"Yeah, usually," I said.

Ms. Marlow opened the sliding door of the van. "Sorry, kids," she said. "I know you prefer the hot and uncomfortable bus."

She gestured for us to climb into the van. Then she said, "Today, you'll have to enjoy the air-conditioned comfort of my personal eight-passenger luxury van. Climb in!"

Gum ran forward. "All right!" he shouted, climbing in. "Whoa, a TV!"

The rest of us shrugged and followed him into the van. It really was a nice van.

"Since we're such a small group, the principal thought it would be a good idea to just take my van," Ms. Marlow explained.

I looked around. "Where's Anton?" I asked.

We looked out the window. Anton came running down the steps of the school. "Hold on!" he yelled. "I'm coming."

"You're a real piece of work, Gutman," Sam said when he got into the van. Sam watches a lot of old movies, so she says weird things sometimes.

"Whatever," Anton said.

"Hey, Ms. Marlow," Cat said. "What is the big crate in the back for?"

I turned in my seat. Way in the back of the van was a big metal crate.

"I have a very big dog, Catalina," Ms. Marlow replied. "That's where he sits when we go on long drives."

"Locked up in a cage?" Cat asked. "Poor guy!"

Ms. Marlow laughed nervously. "Yes, I know," she said. "I hate it too. But if I don't put him in there, he comes up front and tries to sit in my lap. It's very dangerous."

The trip in Ms. Marlow's van was awesome. We watched TV, played video games, and had a great time the whole way. It felt like the quickest trip ever.

Before we knew it, we were at the zoo.

MONORAIL

"Whoa, look at that!" Cat said when we got out of the van. She pointed up toward the sky over the zoo.

I turned to look. Right away, I picked up my camera. That was worth a photo. It was like a train from the future, soaring over the whole zoo!

"Pretty crazy, isn't it?" Ms. Marlow said. "The zoo spent millions on that new monorail."

Gum shielded his eyes and stared at the monorail. "It is pretty cool," he said.

Cat scratched her head. "Millions?" she asked. "That seems like a lot."

Ms. Marlow nodded. "It is a lot," she agreed. "The zoo could have spent it on improving some of these animals' living spaces."

I glanced at Cat. From the look on her face, I could tell Ms. Marlow's words made her feel sad.

"Are you okay, Cat?" I asked quietly.

Cat nodded. "Yeah," she said. "I just always thought this zoo was pretty good for the animals here."

I wanted to say something, but I wasn't sure how to make her feel better.

Just then, a woman in tan shorts and a tan shirt came over to us. She looked like she just got back from a safari. I took a quick photo of her.

"Hello, kids!" the woman said. "Is this the science club?"

We all nodded.

"In that case," the woman replied, "I'm Shari, your guide. And I have a treat for you."

Cat stepped forward. "Island Foxes?" she asked excitedly.

Shari laughed. "Soon," she replied. "First, though, we'll have a superspeed tour of the zoo."

"Superspeed?" I asked. "Were we supposed to bring our running shoes?"

Shari smiled at me. "Of course not," she replied. "We'll be seeing everything from above, from the new monorail!"

"Yes!" Anton said. "That thing is awesome."

Gum nodded. "For once, I have to agree with you, Anton," he said. "This should be way cool."

Of course, I agreed. I mean, imagine the pictures you could take from up there. But when I looked at Cat and Ms. Marlow, I could see that not everyone was pleased.

"It'll be fun, Cat," I said as we followed Shari to the monorail entrance.

Cat shrugged. "I guess so," she replied. "I just feel bad if the zoo really did use money that could have helped the animals."

Soon we were high above the zoo. Cat sat next to Ms. Marlow. "Ms. Marlow," Cat said, "I thought this zoo was good for the animals. Don't most of the animals have lots of room to run and play?"

The monorail glided over a big expanse of grass and trees and hills. A golden lion was lounging in the grass. He seemed very relaxed and happy. I took a photo, of course.

Suddenly Gum jumped to his feet. He shouted, "Look at that!"

"Please stay seated," Shari said. We all looked out the window, trying to see what Gum was shouting about.

A huge group of people was marching around in front of the zoo. They were carrying signs and chanting. We couldn't hear what they were saying, though.

"Who are they?" I asked.

"Those are protestors," Ms. Marlow said. "It looks like the Animal Protectors, or the AP."

"You know them, Ms. Marlow?" Cat asked. She sounded like she wished she could join them.

"Yes," Ms. Marlow said. "When I was in college, I was the head of my local chapter of the AP."

"Not anymore?" I asked. I turned in my seat to take a few pictures of the protestors.

Ms. Marlow shook her head. "No," she said. "I left the group after college. It took up too much of my time."

"What are they protesting?" Sam asked.

The monorail took a sharp curve. Ms. Marlow pointed down to the gorilla area.

"My guess is they're protesting things like that cage," Ms. Marlow said. "See that big gorilla?"

We all looked down. A few gorillas were gathered on a small hill near a fake pond. The hill was surrounded on all sides by a heavy fence-like cage.

In the middle of the hill was the biggest gorilla. He had a gray back. The other gorillas were all black.

"That big one," Ms. Marlow said, "is a silverback. That means he's the oldest and strongest male. He's the leader."

"He's huge," Anton said. "Why is he just sitting there? Shouldn't he be beating his chest or something?"

Cat rolled her eyes. "Gorillas only do that if another gorilla is challenging them, or if there's danger," she said. "That gorilla isn't being challenged."

Shari smiled. "That's right!" she said. "I see we have an animal lover here."

Cat beamed. "I really love animals," she said.

Ms. Marlow frowned. "I wish whoever built that cage loved animals," she said quietly.

"What's wrong with the gorilla cage?" I asked. "They look happy and relaxed."

Ms. Marlow shook her head slowly. "To me they look sad and bored," she said. "Look at the size of the cage."

"Is it too small?" Cat asked.

The monorail began to slow down. It was pulling into a station.

"Much too small," Ms. Marlow replied. "One troop of gorillas in the wild should have a territory as big as twenty-five square miles."

"Wow," Gum said. "That's as big as . . ."

"This whole zoo," Cat suggested.

"Bigger than that," Sam added.

The monorail screeched to a halt. We started to get off.

Ms. Marlow and Shari led us off the platform. "Actually, our entire town is about twenty-five square miles," Ms. Marlow said.

Shari smiled nervously. "Anyway," she said, "let's head to the Island Foxes!"

"Finally!" Cat said. I could tell she was excited to see the foxes.

Of course, when my friends and I go on a field trip, nothing is ever what we expect.

ED MARS

We followed close behind Shari and Ms. Marlow. Cat, Sam, and Gum huddled around me as we walked. I was looking through the pictures I'd taken from the monorail.

There were pictures of the gorillas, and some of the lions. Plus, I had gotten some great shots of the protestors.

Sam grabbed my hand. "Wait a second, Egg," she said. "Go back to that last photo."

I clicked the back button on my camera.

"That one!" Sam said. "Who is that?"

It was a picture of an older man. He was balding, but had a long gray ponytail. He was wearing a dirty red T-shirt and waving a sign.

"I don't know," I replied. "He's a protestor, I guess."

Sam stroked her chin. "I know that mug from someplace," she said. "Mug means face," she added quickly.

She thought a minute. Suddenly she snapped her fingers. "That is Ed Mars," she said. "He's a famous animal rights protestor. I read about him in a magazine."

Ms. Marlow stopped walking. "Ed Mars?" she said. "Was he at the protest?"

Sam nodded. "I'm sure it was him," she said.

Ms. Marlow said, "Wow. He's an idol of mine, in a way. He's done great things for animals over the years."

Sam frowned. "Wasn't he arrested recently?" she asked. "I think my grandpa was watching it on the news last week."

Ms. Marlow waved her hand. "Yes," she said. "Ed got in trouble for breaking into a laboratory and rescuing some monkeys."

Cat looked very upset to hear about the monkeys in the laboratory. But just then, Shari came to a stop.

"Uh oh," Shari said. "This doesn't look good."

We all jogged up to gather around Shari. "What's going on?" Sam asked.

We were at the Island Fox exhibit, but no other visitors were around. Instead, it was swarming with zookeepers and police!

I snapped a few pictures right away.

Shari walked over to a man in a tan zoo uniform like hers. He was talking to the police.

When he saw Shari, the man shook his head. "This is bad, Shari," the zookeeper said.

"What happened?" our guide asked. "Aren't the foxes okay?"

The man took a deep breath. "I'm afraid I don't know," he said.

Shari looked confused. "What do you mean?" she asked. "Aren't we opening the exhibit today? These students are from the middle school science club. They're here to see the foxes."

The zookeeper sighed. "They won't see them today," he said. "The foxes have been stolen!"

CHAPTER SIX

SUSPECTS

Ms. Marlow and Shari went to talk to the police. They sent us to the snack stand. On our way, Cat, Gum, Sam, and I had our picture taken with a goat. Then we sat around a white plastic table.

We were all enjoying some ice cream. Gum's chewing gum was safely stored on the end of his nose to finish after the snack.

It didn't take long for Sam to come up with a suspect.

"I guess we all know **who** the foxnapper is," she said.

"We do?" Cat asked. "I have no idea who the foxnapper is."

Gum nodded slowly. "Of course we do!" he said. "It's so obvious."

I thought about it for a second. Who could it have been?

Then it hit me. "Aha!" I said. "It must have been Ed Mars."

Cat frowned. "I don't know," she said slowly.

"Why not?" I asked. "Sam said he had been arrested before for monkeynapping."

Sam shook her head. "No, no," she said. "I don't think it was Ed Mars."

I was shocked. "You don't?" I asked. "But he's the perfect suspect."

"I know who it is," Gum said. "I'm sure of it."

Sam cut him off. "It was Ms. Marlow," she said.

We all practically fell over. "Ms. Marlow?" Cat cried. "Are you serious?"

Sam smiled. "I'm sure of it," she said. "She obviously hates this zoo."

She did seem to hate it. "Do you think she took the Island Foxes so that she can free them?" I asked.

Sam nodded. "Plus," she went on, "she has that huge crate in her van."

Cat shook her head. "That's for her dog," she said. "She told us!"

"A likely story," Sam replied. "I don't believe it."

Gum said, "Maybe it was Ed Mars, and maybe it was Ms. Marlow, but I doubt it."

"Who do you think it was?" I asked.

"Who's missing from this table?" Gum replied.

Cat, Sam, and I looked around. "This is all of us," Cat said.

It wasn't all of us. "Anton!" I said, jumping to my feet. "Anton Gutman is missing!"

FOX HUNTER

Gum finished his ice cream and started chewing his gum again. "Anton is missing. The foxes are missing," he said. "Anton must have taken them."

"But why would Anton want the foxes?" I asked. "Ed Mars and Ms. Marlow both seem to have motives."

Gum shook his head. "Anton Gutman never needs a motive," he said.

Cat nodded. "His motive is being a pain," she said. "Ed Mars and Ms. Marlow love animals. They wouldn't steal the foxes."

Gum pointed at Cat. "She's right," he said. "The foxes are being helped here."

We sat quietly and thought about it. Soon we heard some adults talking.

"Listen," Sam whispered. She's great at spying.

I glanced over. A few feet from us, two adults were talking loudly.

One of the adults was a woman. She was wearing a zoo uniform. The other person was an older man. He had a big white mustache and was wearing a huge cowboy hat.

"I don't care
if the foxes
were stolen.
I still have to get paid, "
the man said.

"I understand that," the woman replied. "You'll get your check."

"The full amount," the man said. His face was red with anger. "Five thousand dollars each!"

"Please, Mr. Moreno," the woman replied. "There's no reason to be upset."

The man took a deep breath. "I apologize for yelling," he said. "But this is my job, ma'am. I caught those foxes with my bare hands."

Mr. Moreno took off his hat and wiped his forehead. "I am sorry the foxes were stolen from the zoo," he added. "But I must get paid for the work I did."

The woman nodded. "Come with me to the accounting office," she said. "We'll get you your check right away."

The two adults headed toward a small building. A sign on its door read "Employees Only."

"Did you hear that?" Sam whispered. "That was the hunter who captured the Island Foxes."

"Did you hear how much they pay him for that?" Gum added. "Five thousand dollars for one little fox. I think I'll become an animal hunter."

"He really wanted that check," Sam said.

I shrugged. "Well, like he said, it's his job," I replied.

Sam looked at me. "True," she said. "Come on. Let's go see what Ms. Marlow and Shari are doing."

We got up to head back to the fox exhibit.

Just then, we saw Detective Jones hurry past. We knew him from some mysteries we'd solved on other field trips.

"Hey, Detective Jones!" I called out.

He stopped and looked back. "Oh, hey," he said, waving. "My junior detectives. Are you trying to find the missing foxes?"

"That's right, Detective," I replied.

The detective nodded. "Good luck," he said. "Whoever cracks the case gets a huge reward. The zoo is offering ten thousand dollars to whoever brings those foxes back."

"Wow!" Cat said.

The detective glanced at his watch. "Well, kids," he said, "I better go. I'm about to go make an arrest."

MORE SPYING

Detective Jones walked away.

My friends and I looked at each other. Then we quickly hurried after Detective Jones.

An arrest? I thought. *Already?*

"Who is he going to arrest?" Cat asked.

Sam shrugged as we ran along. "I guess we're going to find out," she said.

Detective Jones stopped at the fox exhibit. Shari and Ms. Marlow were still there.

"Where's Ed Mars?" the detective demanded. "I hear he's been hanging around here."

Shari and Ms. Marlow glanced at each other. "Ed Mars was out in front earlier," Shari replied. "He and his organization were protesting again."

"Protesting, huh?" the detective said. "Against what? Something about the foxes?"

"No, not the foxes," Ms. Marlow replied. "The Animal Protectors are protesting the gorillas' small living space."

Shari frowned. "It's true," she said. "The gorillas' space is too small. The AP likes to remind us."

"Hmm,"
the detective said.

"And Mars
hasn't been seen at
the fox exhibit
today?"

"Not that I know of," Shari replied.

Just then, I heard someone giggling nearby. I tugged Gum's shirt and turned toward the sound of laughter.

Anton was trying to sneak past us behind some bushes.

"Let's follow him," Gum said.

As quietly as we could, Gum and I headed after Anton. Sam and Cat were right behind us.

Then Gum stepped on an empty water bottle. It crinkled loudly, and Anton turned and saw us. He took off like a shot.

"Get him!" Cat shouted.

We chased Anton around the curvy paths of the zoo. He ran past the snack bar and the employee building.

We were getting closer. Then he made a sharp turn past the reptile house.

"That way," Sam said, pointing.

We turned the corner as fast as we could. We didn't see Anton anymore, but we nearly ran into Mr. Moreno, the animal hunter!

PET MOUSE

Mr. Moreno had his back to us, so he didn't see us.

"Look!" Sam whispered.

"It's the hunter!" Gum whispered. "He's not alone."

We instantly jumped behind a bush to watch the hunter and another man. The hunter was holding his paycheck. "Ten thousand smackeroos," he said.

"When do I get my share?" the other man said. "As your assistant, I get twenty percent, don't forget."

"I know, Toro, I know," the hunter replied. "As soon as this check clears, you'll get your money."

"I better," the assistant said. He slipped his hand into his jacket pocket and then immediately pulled it back out.

"Ouch!" Toro shouted. "Stupid mouse! He bit me!"

He reached back into his pocket and pulled out a mouse.

Cat nearly squealed. Sam had to cover her mouth so we wouldn't be caught.

"I love mice!" Cat whispered.

"Shh," Gum said.

"What are you doing with that mouse in your pocket?" Mr. Moreno asked Toro.

I used my zoom lens to snap a quick shot of the little mouse. It was an ordinary brown mouse. It seemed to be trying to escape.

Toro quickly slipped the mouse back into his pocket. "This mouse?" he said. "Why, this is my pet mouse, of course."

"Pet mouse?" Mr. Moreno asked. "I never heard of you having a pet mouse."

"Sure," Toro replied quickly. "His name is, um, Mr. Squeakers."

"What a cute name!" Cat whispered to me.

"Let's get to the bank and cash this check," Mr. Moreno said. "You can play with your mouse later."

"I'll catch up with you," Toro said. "I have some things to do."

"Fine," the hunter replied. "Meet me at the truck in fifteen minutes."

The two man shook hands. Then they walked off in opposite directions.

"That assistant is really odd," Gum said. "He seems sneaky. And also, who keeps their pet mouse in their pocket? That's really weird, if you ask me."

"I agree," I said.

Cat shrugged. "I don't know," she said. "If I had a pet mouse, I'd keep her in my pocket."

Sam shook her head. "You're a piece of work, Cat," she said. "A real piece of work."

We stepped out from behind the bush. Suddenly, though, we were all flat on our backs. Anton had run right into us!

"Aha!" Sam said. "Gotcha!"

WHAT FOXES?

We were all in a pile on the ground. Anton stood up first and wiped the dirt from his pants.

"Okay, okay," he said. "You don't have to knock us down."

That's when I saw that Anton wasn't alone. He was with two of his weaselly friends.

"What are you two doing here?" I asked as I got up and made sure my camera wasn't cracked.

"I told them to meet me here," Anton said. "Hey, I don't mind going to the zoo, but I'd rather hang out with my friends than with you dorks."

"So you didn't steal the foxes?" Gum asked.

"The foxes?" Anton said. "What foxes?"

Sam rolled her eyes. "The Island Foxes!" she said. "You know, the reason we're at the zoo?"

"Oh right," Anton replied with a shrug. "Those foxes. What happened to them?"

"They were stolen, you banana," Cat replied. "Where have you been?"

"We were looking at the snakes," Anton said. "And now we're going to get some ice cream. So bug off."

After that, Anton and his sidekicks walked off, laughing.

"I guess he didn't steal the foxes," I said.

"Where does that leave us?" Gum asked.

Sam sighed and said, "No closer to finding the foxes, I guess."

MORE SPYING

The four of us walked slowly back to Ms. Marlow's van. It was time to head back to school.

"I can't believe this," I said.

"I was so sure it was Anton this time," Gum said sadly.

"You always think it's Anton," Sam pointed out.

"That's true," Gum admitted.

"He was missing and everything," Cat said. "I thought it was Anton too."

As we walked, I clicked through the pictures I had taken on the trip. Then I stopped for a moment on the pictures of Mr. Moreno and his assistant, Toro.

Suddenly, I stopped in my tracks.

"Guys," I said. "I know who took the foxes."

"Is your suspect Ed Mars?" Sam asked.

I shook my head. "Nope," I said.

"It was Ms. Marlow!" Gum said. "That cage in the van was a clue. I bet the foxes are in it right now!"

We were already at the van. I ran over to the back door and pulled it open. The cage was still there, and it was empty.

Gum scratched his head. "Okay, I guess not!" he said.

I smiled. "I knew the cage would be empty," I said.

Ms. Marlow was saying goodbye to our guide, Shari, and to Detective Jones. "Thanks for showing us around, Shari," she said. "And Detective, I hope you find that crook."

"Ms. Marlow?" I said, walking over to them.

"Yes, Edward?" Ms. Marlow replied. "What is it? We need to get you kids back to school."

"First we need to find Mr. Moreno, the animal hunter," I said.

"Mr. Moreno?" Sam asked. "He stole the foxes?"

I shook my head.

"Nope. But he can help us find the man who did."

Shari and Ms. Marlow looked at Detective Jones. "These kids are great at solving mysteries," Detective Jones said. "We should listen to them. Do you know where we can find Mr. Moreno?"

"Mr. Moreno parks his truck in the employee lot," Shari said. "This way."

We all followed Shari. She led us around the back of the zoo. As we got to the parking lot, a bright orange SUV was pulling out.

"Mr. Moreno!" Shari yelled. "Please wait!"

"Now what?" Mr. Moreno replied as he stopped the pickup. "Don't tell me you want your money back."

"Of course not," Shari replied.

"Where is your assistant, Mr. Moreno?" I asked.

"Toro?" Mr. Moreno replied. "He's in the back of the truck. We're on our way to the bank now to cash my check."

My friends and I ran to the back of the SUV and pulled open the tailgate.

"Hey, what's going on?" Mr. Moreno said. He jumped out of the driver's seat.

The tailgate opened with a loud squeak. There, squatting in the back of the little truck, was Toro. Next to Toro was a crate with airholes in it.

"What do you want?" Toro asked. He was holding a little mouse.

"What are you doing with that mouse?" Cat asked angrily.

"My guess is he's about to drop it into that crate," I said.

Shari looked at me, then at the mouse. "Aha," she said. "That's not just a mouse. It's supper."

"Supper?" Mr. Moreno said. "Wait a second, Toro, you told me that was your pet mouse. Mr. Squeakers."

"And what animal likes to eat mice for supper?" I asked.

"Island Foxes," Detective Jones said. He leaned forward and opened the crate.

Two small foxes were inside. They huddled together at the back of the crate.

Detective Jones grabbed Toro by the arm and pulled him out of the truck. "You're under arrest," the detective said.

"I don't get it, Toro," Mr. Moreno said. "Why did you steal the foxes you helped to catch in the first place?"

"Isn't it obvious?" Toro replied. "I did it for the money."

"But you got paid for catching the foxes to begin with," Cat pointed out.

"Not enough, though," I said. "Right?"

Toro sneered. "I do all the work on our hunts," he said. "And I get hardly any of our pay."

"But if you turned in the stolen foxes, you'd get the $10,000 reward," I added.

"It was the perfect plan," Toro said. "Until you kids ruined it for me."

Detective Jones put Toro into a nearby police car and closed the door.

"Well, Shari," the detective said, "you got your foxes back."

"Thanks to the science club," Shari replied.

"I'm going to take this crook downtown and book him for foxnapping," the detective said.

"Don't forget attempted mouse murder!" Cat added with a laugh.

Just then, Anton walked up. "There you guys are," he said. "I've been waiting at Ms. Marlow's van forever."

"Anton," Ms. Marlow said, "your friends caught the man who stole the foxes."

Anton looked at me, Sam, Cat, and Gum. "What foxes?" he asked. "And besides, these dorks are not my friends."

"What are you going to do with the reward money?" Shari asked me.

I looked at my friends. "I think we'll donate it to the zoo," I said. "To make the gorilla cage bigger."

Cat smiled. Then we headed back to Ms. Marlow's van.

The field trip was over. Another mystery was solved.

literary news

MYSTERIOUS WRITER REVEALED!

▶ SAINT PAUL, MN

Steve Brezenoff lives in St. Paul, Minnesota, with his wife, Beth, their son, Sam, and their small, smelly dog, Harry. Besides writing books, he enjoys playing video games, riding his bicycle, and helping middle-school students work on their writing skills. Steve's ideas almost always come to him in his dreams, so he does his best writing in his pajamas.

arts & entertainment

CALIFORNIA ARTIST IS KEY TO SOLVING MYSTERY – POLICE SAY

Early on, C. B. Canga's parents discovered that a piece of paper and some crayons worked wonders in taming the restless dragon. There was no turning back. In 2002 he received his BFA in Illustration from the Academy of Arts University in San Francisco. He works at the Academy of Arts as a drawing instructor. He lives in California with his wife, Robyn, and his three kids.

A Detective's Dictionary

advisor (ad-VYE-zor)–someone who leads and helps a group

arch nemesis (ARCH NEM-uh-sis)–the person with whom you fight the most

arrest (uh-REST)–to stop and hold someone by the power of law

assistant (uh-SISS-tuhnt)–someone whose job is to help someone else

idol (EYE-duhl)–someone who is loved and admired by someone else

junior (JOO-nyur)–younger

motive (MOH-tiv)–a reason for committing a crime

organization (or-guh-nuh-ZAY-shuhn)–a group

protestor (PROH-test-ur)–someone who publicly and strongly objects to something

suspect (SUH-spekt)–someone who may be responsible for a crime

Stolen Animals

When we were at the River City Zoo, some Island Foxes were stolen. They might have been the first Island Foxes ever stolen, but they were not the first animals ever taken from a zoo. In fact, many rare animals have been stolen from zoos.

People steal animals from zoos for many different reasons. They may want to sell the animal, if it is a very rare animal. They may want to use the animal's fur, skin, or bones to make money. Sometimes people steal animals as a form of protest.

A zoo in Devon, England, was stolen from twice over a two-month period in 2004. During the first theft, five spider monkeys were taken. The second theft was of ten monkeys, including a baby monkey and its parents. Zookeepers suspected that the animals were being sold in Europe.

Baby monkeys were stolen from another Devon zoo in 2006. Those monkeys were only the size of a human thumb. When fully grown, they were about 7 inches tall.

In 2008, a Sao Paulo, Brazil, zoo reported the theft of seven rare albino alligators. The alligators were each worth almost ten thousand dollars. The zookeepers were sure that the animals were being sold since they were worth so much money. The zookeepers were really worried about the animals. Since the alligators were so light in color, it would be bad for them to be in direct sunlight.

The theft of animals has happened for a long time, but people shouldn't steal animals from zoos.

Great job, Egg. I think it would be kind of cool to have a thumb-sized monkey, but I don't want to steal one! — Mr. N.

FURTHER INVESTIGATIONS
CASE #FTM03EG

1. In this book, Ms. Marlow took our science club on a field trip to the zoo. Where have you gone on a field trip? If you could go anywhere on a field trip, where would you choose to go?

2. Why did Toro steal the Island Foxes? What could he have done instead?

3. Gum, Cat, Sam, and I made a list of suspects to solve this mystery. Think of a mystery that needs to be solved at your school or home. Working as a group, make a list of suspects. Then solve the mystery!

POLICE LINE DO NOT CR

IN YOUR OWN DETECTIVE'S NOTEBOOK . . .

1. I love photography. Choose your favorite hobby and write about it. Don't forget to include why you chose that hobby as your favorite.

2. My best friends and I do lots of things together. Write about your best friend. What do you like to do together?

3. This book is a mystery story. Write your own mystery story!

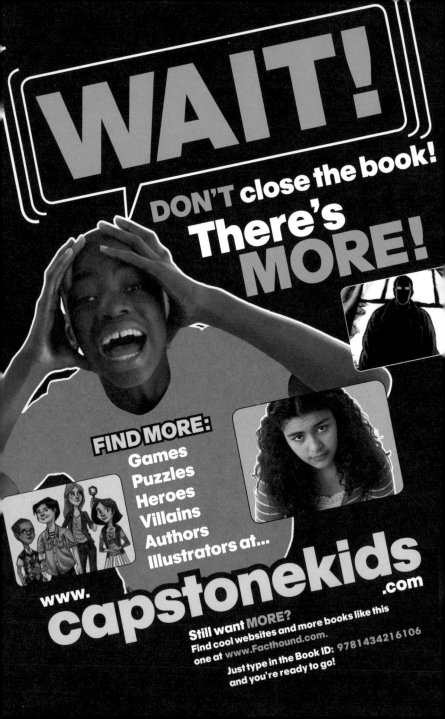